Polly
Pomegra...

Belinda
Blackcurr...

Alice Apple

Peter
Potato

Grace Grape

Wee Willie
Water Melon

The Garden Gang
Stories and pictures by
Jayne Fisher

Other Garden Gang stories

Series 793

Sheila Shallot

Ladybird Books Loughborough

Sheila Shallot
had a vivid imagination.
She was always
telling stories
but nobody believed her.
She really wanted
to go to school
like all her friends,
but because she wasn't
old enough,
poor Sheila had to
stay at home,
and her mother
was always too busy
to play with her.

Sometimes she would
sit on a large stone
at the bottom
of the garden,
watching the bees
buzz merrily in and out
of the flowers.
But she couldn't play
with the bees.
She often listened to
the sweet song
of the birds
in the apple trees
but she couldn't
talk to them.
So Sheila decided
to talk to herself.

Every day she would sit
in her favourite corner
of the garden
talking and talking.
Her mother
would look out
of the window
and sigh,
''She is talking
to herself again,
but at least it
keeps her occupied.''
Sheila's chatter
went on
from dawn till dusk.

But the next morning,
to Sheila's amazement,
she found a fairy
sitting on her stone.
"Hello," said the fairy.
"H . h . . hello," said Sheila,
"I didn't know
there were real fairies."
"Well, there are,"
said the fairy.
"And I didn't realise
there were real
Fruit and Vegetable people."

Sheila talked merrily
to her new friend.
Once, when Miss Delia
Damson passed
she asked, "Who are you
talking to, dear?"
"A fairy," Sheila told her.
Delia went away laughing.
Poor Sheila,
she couldn't understand
why Miss Delia Damson
had laughed at her.

The same thing happened
when several other people
wondered why Sheila
was merrily talking
to nobody in particular.
Their laughter
made Sheila
begin to wonder
if her lovely little fairy
was really there.
She waved goodbye
and went slowly
up the garden path.
''I'm sure she is,''
Sheila said to herself.

"I don't care
what people think,
I know my fairy
is there,"
muttered Sheila
to herself,
as she trotted
down the garden
the following morning.
She played happily
in the sunshine
with her little friend
until lunch time.
Then she hurried home
to wash her hands
and make herself
look tidy.

"I had a lovely
game of ball
with my fairy today,"
said Sheila
at the dinner table.
"And we played
hide and seek."
Her mother just
looked strangely
at her
and smiled.
"Finish your lunch
or there will be no
icecream," she said.
Her father
said nothing.

As soon as the meal
was over,
Sheila suddenly
grabbed her father's hand
and hurriedly led him
down the garden.
"I know he will believe me
even if the others don't,"
she thought.
"Daddy, look through
the bushes
and you will see
my fairy," she said.
"She's gone home
for lunch," he said.

Sheila was looking
very cross
as she went down
to her stone the next day.
"What's the matter?"
said the familiar voice
of her fairy.
"Nobody believes in you,
except me," said Sheila.
"Well," said the fairy,
"tonight, after dark,
they will see."

"We'll never hear
the last of it
if we don't go,"
said Sheila's mother,
as her daughter
led them carefully
down the garden path
after dark.
"Look through
the bushes," said Sheila.
They all peered through
and to their amazement
saw, not one but about
thirty, fairies dancing.
"Good gracious,"
they all said,
"she really . . .

25

didn't
make it up!

Benny
Broad Bean

Benny Broad Bean
was a real boy bean.
He loved the garden
and took a great interest
in everything
that went on there.
The birds, the insects,
the worms and the grubs,
he knew them all by name,
and they all knew him.

You can imagine
his surprise then,
when one morning
early in spring
he came across some
horrible looking jelly
in the small
garden pond.
It was a cluster
of round jelly balls
with black dots
in the middle.
"Ugh!" he thought.
"I wonder who put
that there. I must keep
an eye on it."

And that is exactly
what he did.
Each morning,
he would peep
into the water
and inspect the jelly.
For several days
nothing happened.
The jelly didn't move
or make a noise.
The goldfish
didn't eat it
and the birds
didn't eat it.
"This certainly
is a mystery,"
thought Benny.

DIARY
B.B.B.

Then one morning,
as he looked
at the jelly,
he noticed that
the black dots
were no longer dots
but long, curved shapes.
"Now this
is interesting,"
thought Benny,
and made a note of it
in his little diary.

A few more days
went by
and another surprise
was in store for him.
The jelly was empty.
Where had all the
black shapes gone?
As he looked closely
he suddenly saw them,
clinging to
the water weeds.
"They are alive,"
he thought
in wonderment.

"Whatever
can they be?"
thought Benny
the next day,
as he watched
the little creatures
begin to move
around the pond,
wriggling what looked
suspiciously like tails.
They fed, wriggled
and sunned
themselves, then
sunned themselves,
wriggled and fed
all over again.

How they grew!
Their heads became bigger,
their tails grew longer,
and their eyes
could be seen quite clearly.
"They are such
happy little things,"
thought Benny,
as he looked at them
lovingly.
"They will be
good company
for the water snails
and the goldfish."

Legs were the next
surprise for Benny.
There they were,
sticking out
from the back
of each
little creature,
a pair of long,
strong legs.
How quickly
they could move
with the help of
their new limbs.
They busily darted
to and fro
in the clear water.

Benny's diary
was becoming very full
because of all the
changes in these
strange creatures.
"Surely they won't
change again,"
he thought.
But they did!
Next came arms, ending
in beautiful hands,
and certainly their tails
were growing shorter.
Benny hardly dared
to leave the pond
in case he missed
anything.

"I don't believe it,"
said Benny out loud
when he looked
into the water one day.
"No tails."
The creatures had
certainly lost their tails
and were scuttling along
in the mud
at the bottom of the pond.
"Whatever next,"
thought Benny.
But the biggest surprise
was yet to come.

The following day,
Benny came to the pond
as usual.
He gazed unhappily
into the water
when he quickly realised
that his precious
creatures had gone.
"Oh dear!" he sighed.
"Now I shall never know
what they were."
Wiping a tear
from his eye,
he turned away, and there
on a stone beside him
sat one of his creatures.
Yes, that's right . . .